OLIVER & DA[

The Search for the Quantum Energizer

BY
ALAN R PETERS

ILLUSTRATED BY
SHIRLEY D WINTER

Copyright Alan R Peters
April 2012

-o-

Published by
The Sevenoaks Publishing Company
www. sevenoakspublishing.co.uk

-o-

Although the main characters in this book
are based on real people, the story
is pure fiction.

-o-

Suggested by an outrageous story, told by one of the
children as an alleged, real life incident and developed
by the author into a full length adventure.

FOREWORD

This is the first in a series of books for young readers, featuring Oliver and Daniel, who are inadvertently drawn into a strange parallel world, where they have to find the missing "Quantum Energizer," before they can return to their own world.

It contains a few words which may be not be known to some young readers. This is a deliberate attempt to improve their vocabulary, rather than substitute simpler words and risk losing the finer meaning of the narrative.

To avoid having to ask an adult for the meaning of these words, a vocabulary is included at the back of the book for easy reference by the reader. Not only will this make life easier for the adults, it is hoped that the young readers will develop the habit of learning the meaning of new words for themselves and, in due course, progress to using a full size dictionary.

The object of the book is, of course, to entertain. If the reader chooses to skim through the more difficult words, without checking their meaning, the author believes that they will still enjoy the story, as did the two boys for whom the story was originally written.

If they use the dictionary at the back of the book, this will be a useful bonus in their education.

Alan Peters
April 2012

CHAPTER 1

One fine day in early spring, Oliver and his young brother Daniel set off to visit their grandparents, who lived just a short distance away. Oliver had made the journey on his own before but this was the first time Daniel had been allowed to go without his parents.

Daniel was very excited and Oliver was feeling very grown up, having to take care of his brother for the first time. He took Daniel's hand as they walked along a short stretch of quiet road, until they arrived at the footpath which they used to cut through to the road where their grandparents lived.

They were halfway down the footpath, which had a high fence on each side, when a very strange thing happened.

A large black bird swooped down from a tree and seized the string of Oliver's yoyo, which was hanging out of his trouser pocket. The bird tugged and the yoyo came out of his pocket before Oliver could do anything to stop it.

Then the bird flew off, over the fence and sat in a tree, just over the boundary.

Oliver was dismayed, because he had only just been given the yoyo and he wasn't going to lose it so soon. Luckily, there was a gate in the fence and Oliver found, to his surprise when he tried the latch, that it was not locked. So he and Daniel went through.

Oliver had always thought that there were people's gardens on the other side of this fence, but what he saw as they went through the gate was very strange.

There was woodland stretching for miles, and off to the right was an enormous lake. It looked like another world. It certainly wasn't someone's garden!

Daniel did not seem to notice how strange the landscape was. He was only interested in getting the yoyo back. Oliver had been letting him play with it before they'd left, and he didn't want him to lose it.

"Let's climb up the tree and get it back," said Daniel, full of positive attitude, but not really thinking through the practical side of climbing the tree, where the lowest branch was well out of reach of either of them.

In any case, what would prevent the bird flying away with the yoyo before they could get to him?

But Oliver was determined to get his yoyo back. He went over to a large wooden box, which must have been thrown over the fence by a fly-tipper, and brought it over to the tree.

By standing on the box, he could just reach the lowest branch and was able, with some difficulty, to pull himself on to it.

It was a good job he'd had a lot of practice climbing trees at his grandparents' house, he thought, otherwise he would have been in trouble!

"I want to come up too," said Daniel, but Oliver was concerned that the bird would fly off if he did not act swiftly.

"I need to get the yoyo back before the stupid bird flies off," said Oliver and turned to check where the bird was.

"I'm not stupid and I'm not going to fly off," said the bird. "I only took your toy to persuade you to come through the gate."

Oliver was astounded. "But birds can't talk," he said, "except parrots, and they don't really understand what they are saying."

"Of course we can talk," said the bird, "it's just that humans can't normally understand us. In this world, it is different. Animals, birds and humans all talk to each other."

"So why did you want us to come through the gate," said Oliver, recovering quickly. Nothing caught Oliver out for long.

He was very quick witted. "What is this place," he asked. "Where are we?"

"I have no idea where we are, or what this place is called," said the bird. "I only know that this is Our World and over the fence is Your World. You will soon find out the differences."

"I will not," said Oliver. "We have to get to our grandparents' house, otherwise they and our parents will wonder where we are. They will be very worried."

"I think," said the bird, which Oliver discovered later was a jackdaw, "that you will not be going to anyone's house soon. Look at the gate."

Oliver looked in the direction in which the jackdaw was indicating, but there was no gate to be seen!

"You can't go back until your job here is done," said the jackdaw. "The gate has closed."

Oliver looked in dismay. The gate had not just closed, it had disappeared completely! They were trapped!

CHAPTER 2

He retrieved his yoyo, which the bird no longer seemed to have any interest in and climbed down from the tree.

"Can I have a go with it?" said Daniel, seemingly oblivious to their dilemma. Oliver passed it to him absentmindedly, still thinking rapidly. How would they get home now?

He turned to look up at the jackdaw. "What must we do," he asked, "to make the gate open again?"

"You must find the missing Quantum Energizer and return it to The Master," he said and promptly flew away.

"Wait," said Oliver becoming alarmed. "Where can we find this Quantum Energizer? What does it look like?"

But Oliver was talking to himself. The jackdaw had gone and they were alone. They were both lost and beginning now to feel just a bit hungry, because it was nearly lunch time.

"I want some chocolate milk," said Daniel "and a cheese sandwich would be good." He would have lived on chocolate milk and cheese sandwiches, if it were left to him, which luckily it wasn't!

Oliver had no idea how they were going to find the Quantum Energizer. He didn't even know what it was! But there was no point staying here.

They had to find something to eat and drink first and worry about the Quantum Energizer later.

So Oliver took Daniel by the hand and they both walked to the lake and started to follow the little path which ran around it.

They had no idea what they would find, or whether they would ever see their parents, grandparents and friends again.

Oliver was very despondent, and to make things worse, Daniel kept asking to be carried!

CHAPTER 3

They had been walking for a while, when they saw, off to the left, a little cottage in a small clearing, overlooking the lake.

"Look," said Daniel, "it's just like our little playhouse house at Granddad's, only bigger."

"It's probably a fishing hut," said Oliver, although he really had no idea what a fishing hut was. He must have read the name somewhere.

"Let's see if there is any porridge in there," said Daniel, whose only experience of little houses, other than the one at Granddad's, was the one in which the three bears lived.

"I hope they aren't at home," he said, looking around nervously.

"I'm sure they won't be," said Oliver.

He tried the door and was surprised when it opened suddenly. There stood a witch, complete with a rather bedraggled, pointed hat, holding a broomstick.

"What do you want," she said, "I'm very busy at the moment."

"Could we have a cheese sandwich and some chocolate milk please," said Daniel. "Ordinary milk will do, if you haven't got any chocolate."

Oliver explained that they couldn't get back home to their own world, because the gate they had come through had closed.

"You had better come in," said the witch, "and I'll see what I can do."

Oliver peered nervously into the dim interior of the house and was amazed how large it was inside. Just inside the door was a coat stand, where several cloaks of different colours were hanging.

A sultry black cat peered at them through half closed eyes and then turned and walked off into the back room. She never spoke.

CHAPTER 4

"Follow me," said the witch and shuffled off towards the door at the back of the hall, which Oliver hoped was to the kitchen.

"It's very dark in here," complained Daniel, but stopped abruptly as the witch turned and glared at him.

Inside the kitchen, the cat had taken up her position next to the fridge. "If there's milk to be had," she spat, "I'm going to be the first in the queue."

Oliver was surprised, even though the jackdaw had said that all animals could talk in this strange world. He gave the cat a weak smile.

"Whatever." said Daniel. He didn't really know what it meant, but his grandmother said it all the time and it just seemed the right thing to say at that moment.

"Would you like some soup?" asked the witch.

"What sort is it?" asked Daniel, who was a bit fussy if things didn't taste of tomatoes or cheese.

"It is toadstool and nettle" said the witch, whose name they had discovered was Minnie. "It's freshly made this morning."

Oliver politely declined. "I think just some bread and jam would be fine," he said.

"Have you got any cheese?" asked Daniel, "and some tomato sauce?"

They finally settled for a boiled egg sandwich and some milk. The cat joined in with her own bowl of milk.

Whilst they ate, they tried to discover exactly what the Quantum Energizer was and where they could find The Master. But Minnie was not much help.

"I have no idea what a Quantum Energizer is," she said, "but I know that our world is shrinking and The Master is trying to find a missing part which powers his machinery. Unless it is found soon, this world will shrink to nothing and will disappear for ever. We are all very worried."

"So where can we find The Master," asked Oliver. "Maybe he can help us with some more information."

"Carry on down the path beside the lake," said Minnie "and you will find his house at the very end of the lake."

"It looks a long way," said Oliver. "I'm not sure Daniel will be able to walk that far. You don't have a spare broomstick we could borrow, do you?" he asked hopefully.

"I'm afraid not," said Minnie, "my old one is being repaired right now and I need the other one every day. But I do have something which might be useful."

She led them outside to a shed and when she opened it, there was a little motor bike at the back.

"I keep this for when my grandson comes to stay," said Minnie, "but it may be too difficult for you to ride."

"Not at all," said Oliver, "I've been riding a bike for years and I'm very good at it. If Daniel holds tightly on the back, I am sure we can manage fine."

"It's only electric powered," said Minnie, "so it will need to be charged up when you get to your destination. I'm sure The Master will be able to recharge it for you for the return journey."

"Can I drive Ollie?" asked Daniel hopefully.

"Maybe later," said Oliver, not really meaning it but just trying to buy a little time. He wasn't even sure if he would be able to balance it with Daniel on the back, but it was worth trying.

There was no way Daniel could walk the whole length of the lake. He would need to be carried before they had travelled a hundred metres! So they each put on their helmets and prepared to leave.

"Thank you so much Minnie," said Oliver, "how can we ever repay you?"

"Just find the missing part and give it to The Master," she said, "and everyone here in Netherworld will be in your debt."

So they set off on their little bike, with Daniel holding tightly on the back.

CHAPTER 5

They were a bit wobbly at first, but most of the time Daniel managed to lean the same way as Oliver. They did fall into some bushes once, and a little later, Oliver managed to brake just as they were about to plunge into the lake.

"You are a very good driver," said Daniel.

"I know," said Oliver, modestly.

Half an hour later, they had covered about half the distance to the end of the lake. They decided to stop for a drink of water, which Minnie had kindly given them, together with a lunch pack.

Daniel wanted a biscuit but Oliver wisely decided they should be saved for another stop a bit further on.

"OK Ollie," said Daniel, being unusually agreeable, "you're in charge."

"Yes," thought Oliver to himself. "This whole mission depends on me and I need to take care of Daniel as well."

Duly refreshed, they started off again down the road. Oliver was becoming very pleased with himself and Daniel was really enjoying the ride.

"This is just like being at the fair," he said. "Go faster Ollie!"

But Oliver knew he should be careful, because Daniel was in his care and his mother would expect it. "It won't go any faster," Oliver lied, and Daniel accepted that.

"OK Ollie," he said, and they drove in silence for a while.

Not far down the road, they spotted a fox limping alongside the track and Oliver slowed and stopped next to him.

Oliver was surprised that the fox didn't run off like foxes usually do. Instead, the fox turned to look at them but said nothing.

He sat down with one front paw lifted off the ground.

"Can I help?" asked Oliver. "You seem to have a limp."

"Yes," said the fox. "I trod on a bramble about a mile back and it's making walking very difficult."

"Let me have a look," said Oliver, getting off the bike and steadying it while Daniel dismounted.

Lifting up the fox's front paw, he looked at the pad.

"Hold still," he said. "I can see a thorn," and he deftly removed it with his thumb and forefinger.

"Is that any better?" he asked.

"Much better," said the fox. "Thank you. Maybe I can help you one day in return. I am Ferdinand, if you need to ask for me."

"Maybe you can help us now," said Oliver. "We are going to see The Master and we have to find something called a Quantum Energizer. You haven't seen one on your travels, I suppose?"

"Sorry," said Ferdinand. "I'm afraid I wouldn't know a Quantum Energizer if I saw one."

"Me neither," said Oliver. "But maybe after we see The Master, we will know more. I hope your paw soon feels better."

They returned to the bike to continue their journey. "Can't we take him with us?" asked Daniel. "I'd like a pet fox."

"Sorry," said Oliver, "there isn't enough room on the bike. Maybe we can collect him on the way back."

"But Ollie,"… started Daniel.

But Oliver was already moving off, heading for The Master's House.

CHAPTER 6

They were nearing the end of the lake but there was still no sign of a house. So the two boys decided to stop for lunch and pulled off the road into a small clearing.

They sat down on a large log in the centre of the clearing and Oliver opened the lunch box. Seemingly out of nowhere, two squirrels appeared and sat on the log opposite them.

"I think they want some lunch," said Daniel.

"Just a biscuit," said one of the squirrels. "We are not too partial to sandwiches, and we are a bit fed up with nuts."

Oliver looked in the box. There were two biscuits each and he decided to share one with the squirrels. He broke one in half and gave them a piece each.

"Thank you," said the one on the left. "I'm Cyril and this is Emily."

"I'm Oliver and this is my brother Daniel," said Oliver.

"We know," said Cyril. "Everyone in Netherworld knows when a stranger enters. We also know that you are looking for the missing Quantum Energizer. But before you ask, we have no idea what it is, or where you can find it. But we both wish you luck."

And with that, they were gone, each clutching a half-eaten biscuit.

"Well," said Oliver, "we aren't having much luck so far, so let's eat lunch and get on our way." So they ate their sandwiches, what was left of the biscuits and drank some of the water.

"We had better be a bit careful with the water," said Oliver. "We may need more before we find The Master's House."

Daniel had finished eating and had wandered off to explore, while Oliver repacked the lunch box. Suddenly, there was a screech from the undergrowth, where Daniel had disappeared, and Oliver dashed in to see what had happened.

He discovered Daniel, pointing at a fence with a gate, just like the one they came through when they first followed the jackdaw.

CHAPTER 7

"Now we can go home," said Daniel, but Oliver was reluctant.

"We have to help these people find the Quantum Energizer first and save their world," he said, "otherwise they will all die."

"I want to see Mummy and Daddy," cried Daniel, "I want to go home!"

Oliver opened the gate to see if it was really an entrance back into their world. He realized immediately that it was, because there were cars all around.

He realized that they had seen no cars in Netherworld so far, so through the gate must be their own world.

"What should he do?" He was undecided. He had been chosen to save Netherworld but it wasn't fair to Daniel to keep him here.

Daniel was too young to understand the importance of finding the Quantum Energizer and save Netherworld.

Oliver made a brave decision. He would take Daniel home and then return to finish the mission. Maybe he could enlist the help of one of his school friends. "That would be good," he thought.

He stepped through the gate with Daniel following. He briefly looked back and saw Daniel on the floor, scraping around as he often did, picking up something which had caught his eye.

He usually ended up with a pocket full of stones and twigs by the time he arrived home!

"Come on Daniel," he said, "and shut the gate, otherwise other people will be wandering in. If it's shut, it looks like it's just a private garden!"

Daniel closed the gate and followed Oliver into what appeared to be a large car park.

"Where are we Ollie?" he said. "It's not where we went in."

"No," said Oliver, "but I know where we are. Look! That's Daddy's car and on that wall it says c-a-r p-a-r-k. We are in the station car park!"

"But how do we get home?" asked Daniel. "Daddy always drives us from here."

"It isn't that difficult," said Oliver. "Look, there is only one way we can get out of this car park," and he started walking briskly up the road towards the exit.

"Carry!" said Daniel. But Oliver was having none of that.

"If you want to see Mummy, you had better keep up," he said sternly and continued walking.

They got to the exit of the car park and they both knew where they were. They were at the end of their grandparent's road and there was a petrol station to the left.

"We turn right here," said Daniel, pointing left.

Oliver said nothing but they turned left, passed the petrol station and a little further on they came to the end of their road.

"Up here," said Daniel, indicating left and soon they were approaching their house from the opposite end of the road to the way they had left.

They finally found number 77, then 79 and then 81. But they lived at 79a! They must have missed it! They looked more carefully but it definitely wasn't there. Where the house should have been, was just a wide garden, which seemed to be part of the house next door.

Oliver was the first to realize what had happened. "Daniel," he said. "What was the car we saw at the station, which we said was Daddy's car?"

"It was a BMW," said Daniel, who could recognize any car at 25 metres, especially if was similar to one owned by someone in the family.

"But Daniel," said Oliver, "Daddy sold the BMW a long time ago and now he's got an Audi."

"Perhaps he's changed back," said Daniel.

"And perhaps he knocked down the house as well," said Oliver, "since we left this morning."

"Don't be silly," said Daniel, but had no further suggestions to make.

Oliver thought furiously. He was familiar with time portals. He had even written a story about one, but he knew they didn't exist in real life. But he could think of no other explanation to account for the situation in which they found themselves!

"We must get back to the gate in the car park Daniel, before it closes," he said. "Otherwise we'll be trapped here, probably before we were even born."

He turned and started to walk down the road towards the station.

"But Ollie", said Daniel, who was not quite as familiar with the concept of time portals as Oliver. He was an ardent Ben 10 fan and more familiar with the concept of aliens than time travel.

"Maybe we have been born, Ollie, but we're still living at the old house. Why don't we go to Nana and Granddad's house and they can drive us there."

"That would be even worse, Daniel. Then there would be two of both of us! No, the only way is to go back through the portal in the car park and try to get back out through the gate we came through in the first place."

Daniel understood even less about a time paradox than he did about time portals, but he trusted his big brother and followed him down the road, back to the station.

They arrived back at the car park and were relieved to see the gate was still there. Oliver turned the handle and it swung open.

"Thank goodness," said Oliver, and they both scuttled through the gate, before it could disappear.

CHAPTER 8

They found the bike where they had left it and were quickly on their way, heading down the side of the lake, to where they were hoping to find The Master's House.

Just when they were thinking they would never find it, there it was! Where the lake ended, was a large house on the right, with outbuildings at the side and rear.

"This is it," cried Oliver. They left the bike outside the main entrance, went in through the side gate and up to the front door.

Daniel reached up and rang the bell rather energetically. Oliver frowned. "I don't suppose he's deaf" he said.

"Sorry Ollie," said Daniel, and they both waited for what seemed an age before they heard someone coming.

The door opened and a little wizened old man, with rimless spectacles and long, wispy grey hair, stood there, blinking at them.

"Is The Master at home?" asked Oliver politely.

"Yes," said the man. "I am The Master. Come inside."

He turned and walked down the hallway, leaving Oliver and Daniel to close the door.

"We didn't tell you who we are," said Oliver politely.

"I know who you are," said the man. "It was I who sent the jackdaw to fetch you in the first place and I have been watching you all the way here."

He beckoned to the two boys to follow him and led them down a long corridor into an enormous room, which he called "The Control Centre."

It was full of strange equipment. People were sitting all around, looking at screens and dials, moving levers and making adjustments to their controls.

"This room contains the equipment which maintains Netherworld," he said. "It keeps it separate from your world and stops it merging back into it.

"It was set up thousands of years ago and was a very small world in the beginning. It has grown, over a long time, to its present size.

"There are now many gateways, each to different parts of your world, in different times," he said. "So we can travel to anywhere in your world, into the past and also into the future.

"This is very useful if something goes wrong in your world. We can go in and correct things before any harm is done, but we try not to do this, except in a real emergency."

Oliver started to ask about Quantum Energizers but The Master interrupted him.

"Six months ago a Quantum Energizer from one of the generators was lost, or stolen. We don't know which.

"The plant is running on reduced power and Netherworld is slowly shrinking. In a few years it will disappear altogether and merge back into your world. Everyone here will die, unless we can find the missing Quantum Energizer and fit it back into the generator."

"What does a Quantum Energizer look like?" asked Oliver.

"Come, I will show you," said The Master, and he took them to where there were eight cylindrical structures, in a semi circle, with a seat in the middle.

He opened the top of one of the cylinders to reveal a shallow, circular recess in the middle. In the recess was what looked like a large, multi-coloured, glass marble.

Different colours swirled around inside it, like a rainbow trying to escape and the whole cylinder hummed quietly. He opened the next cylinder but the recess was empty.

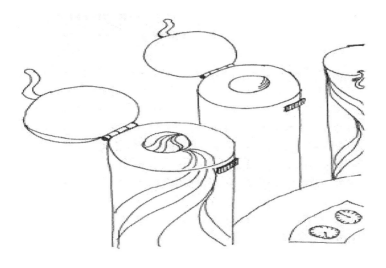

"This one is missing," he said. "Only seven remain. We must find the missing one quickly, before it is too late."

"That's easy," said Daniel, who had not seemed to be taking much notice of what was happening until now.

Oliver and The Master both looked at him in amazement, as he pulled a large glass marble from his pocket. "You can use this one," he said.

"Don't be silly Daniel," said Oliver. "That's just one of your old marbles from home."

Without saying anything, Daniel stepped up to the console and dropped the marble into the empty recess. Immediately the marble began to glow, and the cylinder began to hum.

"Where did you get that?" shrieked Oliver and The Master together.

"When we went through the gate to go back home, it was on the ground just inside," said Daniel, "and I picked it up."

You were in a bit of a hurry Ollie, so I just put it in my pocket and forgot about it!"

Oliver could not believe it, but it was obviously the missing part.

He was a bit upset that it was Daniel who had solved the problem and not him, but he was also relieved that Netherworld would now be saved and they could both go home.

Suddenly he remembered that the gate through which they had entered had closed. But didn't the jackdaw say it would be opened when they completed their task?

He asked The Master about the closed gate. "How will we get out of Netherworld," he said.

"On the way back to return your bike, ask Minnie and she will arrange for the gate to be opened," he said, "just as jackdaw promised. She will also have a small gift for you to reward you for all your help."

"What," asked Daniel, "like some chocolate eggs or marshmallows? I really like marshmallows, especially in a chocolate milkshake!"

"You will have to wait and see Daniel," said The Master with a smile. "Without you two, Netherworld would soon have ceased to exist, so your reward will be much more than a few chocolate eggs! Now, let's have some lunch before you set off. It will take you some time to get back."

CHAPTER 9

Oliver and Daniel were soon on the little path running alongside the lake, on their way back to the gate where they hoped to get back into their own world.

Daniel was excited and impatient and so was Oliver, although he tried to control his curiosity. Not so Daniel.

"What do you think our present will be?" he asked for the third, or fourth time.

"I don't know," said Oliver, "but the quicker we get to Minnie's house, the sooner we will know."

"Go faster," said Daniel, but Oliver wasn't going to risk an accident now, just to get back a few minutes earlier.

It seemed a shorter journey going back and soon they could see Minnie's cottage in the distance.

A few minutes later, they were knocking on Minnie's door. The cat watched them through her narrow, yellow eyes, but said nothing.

Minnie opened the door with a towel in one hand and a wooden spoon in the other. She looked quite homely without her hat.

"Oh, it's you, Oliver and Daniel," she said. "Do you want some soup?"

"No thank you," said Oliver. "We came to return your bike. We have completed our mission and The Master said you would open the gate for us."

"And give us a present," said Daniel excitedly.

"Come in," said Minnie, and she turned back into the dim interior of the cottage, followed by the two boys and the cat.

"Now," said Minnie. "I am instructed to give you this."

She handed Oliver a small rectangular box, about the size of a match box, with two buttons on it.

"As you approach the fence," she said, "first press this button on the left. A small aerial will come out of the box and the outline of the gate will appear.

"When you are close enough, press the second button and the gate will become solid. You will then be able to open it and step through. The gate will automatically close and disappear one minute later, so make sure you go straight through."

"And what present have you got for us?" said Daniel. "A yoyo would be good, so I wouldn't have to borrow Ollie's."

"The present for all your help, is the Portal Opener," said Minnie. "You can keep it to use whenever you want to come back. It also opens gates to other times, as you have already seen, so you will have to be very careful how you use it.

"One more thing," she said. "When you go back through the gate, it will be exactly the same time as when you left, so no one will have missed you. Go straight to where you were going before you came in through the gate."

"Thank you Minnie," said Oliver. "We hope we will see you again."

They both set off towards the fence which they could see in the distance.

"I would have liked some sweets as well," complained Daniel, as they left. But Oliver reminded him they would be getting sweets where they were going and Daniel perked up.

"Let's go Ollie," he said.

Oliver used the Portal Opener and sure enough, the gate appeared in the fence. He pressed the second button, stepped up to it, turned the handle and they both went through.

CHAPTER 10

Once through the gate, they set off towards their grandparent's house, still wondering if everyone would be worried where they had been. But Oliver remembered what Minnie had said.

"Daniel," said Oliver. "When we get there, pretend we came straight here, ok?"

"Ok Ollie, but can we tell them about the jackdaw?"

"I suppose that wouldn't hurt," said Oliver

They covered the short distance to their grandparents' house very quickly. But as soon as they got to the gate at the top of the drive, Oliver knew something was terribly wrong.

Instead of the smart, wrought iron gates with brick pillars, there was a derelict five-bar wooden gate, hanging off broken wooden posts.

Halfway down the drive, a Lassie-type dog came bounding up to greet them, its tail wagging furiously.

"What's happened Ollie?" said Daniel. "Nana doesn't have a dog!"

"I don't know," said Oliver, "but we had better be careful. I think we might have come through the wrong gate. Maybe into the wrong time! It seems to be before the new gates were built, so Nana and Granddad may not even live here yet!"

The dog ran ahead of them, did a complete circuit of the house at full speed and then disappeared into the open back door.

Oliver and Daniel followed the dog and carefully peered into the kitchen from the back door. The dog sat panting in her basket, looking hopefully at the boys. She just wanted to play!

The kitchen didn't look the same as usual. Instead of white doors, there were dark wooden ones, and where the table should have been was a breakfast bar.

Nana was there, but she wasn't on her iPad, as she was usually. She was sitting at the breakfast bar, reading a newspaper. She looked up as the boys nervously came into the room.

"Hello boys," she said. "Who are you?"

"We are Oliver and Daniel," said Daniel. "We are…." But Oliver knew what had happened and cut him short.

"We are from down the road," he said, quite truthfully "and we are looking for our friend who lives around here somewhere. I think we might be in the wrong house!"

"I think you are, but come in and tell me who you are looking for," said Nana. "I might be able to help. Sheba won't bite" she said, nodding towards the panting dog in the basket.

They both went into the kitchen. Oliver thought that Nana looked much younger than when they were here just a short while ago, and he couldn't see Granddad anywhere.

"What is your friend's name?" asked Nana.

The question caught Oliver by surprise. He hadn't thought that one through carefully enough!

He answered with the first names which came into his head, which were the names of the children, his very good friends, who lived there in the time he came from.

"William," he said. "His name is William and he has a sister called Izzie."

"I don't know of anyone with that name around here," said Nana. "It must be someone who only just moved in."

Just then, a young man aged about 17, came through into the kitchen and Oliver and Daniel both gaped. They recognized him instantly from photos they had seen. It was their father. But he was so young!

"This is Christopher," said Nana.

"We know," said Daniel, "we've seen his photograph."

"It's up on the wall," added Oliver quickly, hoping that Nana would overlook the fact that they knew his name.

Christopher was in a hurry. It seems he was off to play cricket. Oliver wished he could go with him. He wished he could tell him who he was, give him a big hug and tell him how they came to be here. But he couldn't. And then he was gone.

"Well," said Nana, "how can we find your friends?"

"We'll look further down the road," said Oliver. "They can't live too far away. We had better be on our way.

"Before Daniel tells all," he muttered to himself.

They said goodbye and then they were out of the door, patting Sheba as they went, and hoping that nothing else embarrassing would happen before they got back to the gate.

CHAPTER 11

When they reached the spot where the Portal should be, they had a problem. If there was more than one gate in that area, how would they choose the right one to go back? Oliver was nervous.

"Ollie," said Daniel. "Why don't we walk up and down the fence and use the Portal Opener to see how many gates we can open. Then we can then look through each one and maybe we will know which one we should use to get back into Netherworld."

"That's a good idea, Daniel," said Oliver, and proceeded to move up and down the pathway, pressing the button on the Portal Opener every so often.

But there was no problem. There only appeared to be one gate from where they were, back into Netherworld, although there was obviously more than one exit from the other side.

So they went through the gate and repeated the exercise from the Netherworld side. There were only two gates leading back out, and since they had just come through one of them, they chose the other one to go back.

CHAPTER 12

They were back in the alleyway, hopefully now in the correct time and set off, once more, to their grandparents' house.

When they reached the entrance gates, they could see that they were back in the right time period. The wrought iron gates were there once more, on the brick pillars, and everything appeared normal.

No dog appeared as they went down the drive and they were a bit sorry about that, because Sheba was such a lovely dog. They wished she could still be here.

They went in through the back door, to the kitchen and there was Nana, as usual, tapping on her iPad.

"How was the journey?" said Nana, as they came in. "No problems I hope?"

"Actually Nana, a strange thing happened on the way here," Oliver began. "A crazy bird came down and took the yoyo from my pocket and flew up into a tree with it."

"Yes," said Daniel, "but Ollie climbed the tree and got it back."

"Whatever," said Nana. She knew Oliver had a very creative imagination. "Would you both like a milkshake?"

"Yes please," said Daniel. "Can I help you make it?"

Oliver thought it best not to tell the rest of the story, because Nana wouldn't believe him anyway. But Nana was looking very thoughtful.

"Do you know, Oliver, just as you walked in, it suddenly reminded me of a visit I had over 20 years ago by two young boys who were very much like you two.

"I can't remember their names, although they did tell me at the time. They were looking for a friend who lived nearby.

"My memory is not what it was, but I do remember who they were looking for. His name was William and now, 20 years later, a William lives in the house next door. Isn't that a strange coincidence?"

"But Nana," said Daniel, "that was us. We went through the wrong time portal, into the past and that's when we came here and met you and Daddy. He was very young…" he tailed off realizing Nana wasn't listening.

"Whatever," she said and continued tapping at her iPad. It seemed that Daniel was fast developing a vivid imagination, just like Oliver.

"Maybe they would both be famous authors when they grew up!" she thought.

Oliver said nothing. He was too busy planning his next trip to Netherworld!

The End

VOCABULARY

(In Alphabetical Order)

Abruptly	Suddenly
Absentmindedly	Without really thinking about it
Alarmed	Frightened
Apparently	It seemed to be
Asked hopefully	He hoped she would say "yes" but didn't really expect her to
Astounded	It was unbelievable
Bedraggled	Untidy, scruffy
Briskly	Quickly
Buy a little time	Put him off until later
Boundary	The fence between the two worlds
Clearing	A space in the woods where there are no trees
Concerned	He was worried
Continued	Carried on
Creative mind	Able to make up stories
Cylindrical	In the shape of a cylinder -look at the picture on page 42 – there are 8 cylinders
Despondent	Losing hope, becoming sad

Dilemma	He had to make a very difficult choice
Dim	Not much light
Dismayed	He was upset and disappointed
Dismounted	Got off the bike
Duly refreshed	After they had rested and eaten something they felt better
Energetically	With lots of energy
Enormous	Very, very large
Exit	The way out
Furiously	He thought very hard and very quickly
Glare	Stare at a bit crossly
Fly Tipper	Someone who throws away rubbish where they should not throw it
Generator	A piece of machinery which makes electricity
Homely	Ordinary – not like a witch
Impatiently	He didn't want to wait
Indicating	Pointing to
Interior	The inside of

Merging	Mixing together
Mission	Something to be done, to be carried out
Modestly	Without being "big-headed"
Multi-coloured	With many colours
Nervously	A little frightened
Oblivious	He didn't notice
Plunge	Fall in head first
Prevent	Stop it happening
Promptly	Straight away
Positive attitude	Behave as if you know you can do it
Quick witted	He always thought very quickly
Rapidly	Quickly
Recess	A hole into which something fits
Retrieved	He got it back
Scuttled	Went through quickly
Semi circle	Half a circle – look at the picture on page 41. The 8 cylinders are arranged in a semi circle.
Shallow	Not very deep
Sternly	Speaking firmly and a little cross; Like Mummy does, when she tells you off.

Sultry	Sulking
Swiftly	Quickly
Tentatively	not being very certain - unsure
Time paradox	Something which seems impossible but has happened because someone has gone back in time
Time portal	A door which takes you to a different time
Unison	All (or both) together
Wizened	Small, wrinkly (old man)

Made in the USA
Charleston, SC
18 September 2012